For JLM, with heartfelt thanks for the inspiration
Bernette Ford

For Bernette, author and editor extraordinaire!
Sam Williams

First published as No More Blanket for Lambkin in North America in 2009 by Boxer Books Limited.

This hardback edition first published in North America in 2014 by Boxer Books Limited.

First published in hardback in Great Britain in 2009 by Boxer Books Limited.

www.boxerbooks.com

The illustrations were prepared using watercolour pans and charcoal on Aquarelle Arches hot press 180lb paper.
The text is set in Adobe Garamond.

ISBN: 978-1-910126-02-8

1 3 5 7 9 10 8 6 4 2

Printed in China

All of our papers are sourced from managed forests and renewable resources.

No More Blanket
for
Little Lamb!

Bernette Ford and Sam Williams

Boxer Books

Ducky knocks on Little Lamb's door. She has come to play.

Little Lamb is hugging her blanket. It is small. It is soft. It is very dirty.

But Little Lamb never lets it go.

"What should we play?"

asks Little Lamb.

Ducky looks around.

Little Lamb has books. She has dolls.

Little Lamb has doll clothes and

ribbons in a little toy chest.

"I want to play laundry day,"
says Ducky.
"Let's do the washing!"
She takes the doll clothes and
marches to the sink.

Ducky climbs up on the stool.

She puts the clothes in soapy water.

"Let's wash the blanket," she says.

"Oh, no," says Little Lamb,

"I can't let my blanket go."

"It's just for a minute," says Ducky.
And she takes Little Lamb's blanket,
and dumps it into the sink!
Little Lamb is very surprised.

But doing the washing

looks like so much fun!

Little Lamb and Ducky

wash and scrub.

Little Lamb and Ducky play

with the soap bubbles.

The soapy water looks dirty.

The clothes look nice and clean.

Off they go, out to the garden.

First, they hang up
the doll's dress and ribbons.

Next, they hang up
the pajamas and socks.

Ducky holds up Little Lamb's blanket.

It is smaller. It is softer.

It is very clean.

But now it has tiny holes.

"Oh, no," Little Lamb cries.

"I want my blanket back!"

"Don't cry," says Ducky.

"We'll let it dry."

The sun dries the clothes.

Little Lamb takes them off the line.

Ducky folds them.

Ducky holds up the blanket.

She ties a ribbon around the middle.

She makes a knot with two corners.

It is small. It is clean.

But it is not a blanket any more.

It's a Little Lamb doll!

"There," says Ducky.

Little Lamb hugs her new little doll.

"No more blanket for Little Lamb!"

she says. "Let's play tea party."

And they do.